381354

D0413486

P1-3

This book is to be returned on or before the last date stamped below.

READING
COLLECTION

16

Library Services
Victoria Buildings
Queen Street
Falkirk

FK2 7AF

F
QUA

Falkirk Council

...rew up in Norfolk, and now misses ...swimming in the river. She has been ...ng life. In 2005 she was shortlisted for ...Fiction Award Having a three-year-old ...er food inspired Katharine to write ...orth London with her two children ...ck cat called Boo.

...on a farm in South Africa and has ...urch minister he went on to a career ...at universities in the Western Cape. ...influenced by his love of travel and ...daughter, both animal-lovers who share ...Piet's first book for Frances Lincoln ...at *Tug of War*. He has also illustrated ...Ravishankar, *All the Wild Wonders* ...recently *Aesop's Fables* by Beverly ...in illustrations at the University of ...Great Malvern with his family.

For my family – and Jay, Max, Anil and Jane too – K.Q

For Elda – P.G.

Fussy Freya copyright © Frances Lincoln Limited 2008
Text copyright © Katharine Quarmby 2008
Illustrations copyright © Piet Grobler 2008

First published in Great Britain in 2008 and in the USA in 2008 by
Frances Lincoln Children's Books, 4 Torriano Mews,
Torriano Avenue, London NW5 2RZ
www.franceslincoln.com

First paperback edition published in Great Britain and in the USA in 2012

All rights reserved

No part of this publication may be reproduced, stored in a retrieval system, or transmitted,
in any form, or by any means, electrical, mechanical, photocopying, recording or otherwise
without the prior written permission of the publisher or a licence permitting restricted copying.
In the United Kingdom such licences are issued by the Copyright Licensing Agency,
Saffron House, 6-10 Kirby Street, London EC1N 8TS.

A catalogue record for this book is available from the British Library.

ISBN: 978-1-84780-045-9

Illustrated with water colours and ink

Set in Missive

Printed in Dongguan, Guangdong, China by Toppan Leefung in December 2011.

1 3 5 7 9 8 6 4 2

Fussy Freya

written by
Katharine Quarmby

illustrated by
Piet Grobler

FALKIRK COUNCIL
LIBRARY SUPPORT
FOR SCHOOLS

FRANCES LINCOLN
CHILDREN'S BOOKS

cucumber

beans (French style)

Spinach

broccoli

Freya had an appetite

as fine as fine could be.

She'd munch up *all* her greens for lunch

and **gobble** fish for tea.

tuna

Freya's mum had cooked a dish
of dhal and jasmine rice.
Baby Ravi ate two bowls,
he liked a bit of spice.

Ravi banged the table-top,
    but Freya sulked and glared –
"Your dhal and rice are just not nice,"
    she suddenly declared.

Her mum first sighed a little
and then she sighed a lot.
Did Freya mind a little?
Not a little, not a jot.

gravy boat (plated silver)

sausage (pork)

bacon
(shoulder)

On Tuesday, Freya spurned a plate
of bacon with baked beans,
and sausages and gravy
and stir-fried winter greens.

winter greens

Mummy scowled a little
and then she scowled a lot.

Did Freya mind a little?
Not a little, not a jot.

The next day, fussy Freya
let out a frightful roar —
"I can't abide your fish!" she cried
and threw it on the floor.

—heirloom

asparagus

parsley

fish knife

Mummy shrieked a little,
Daddy shrieked a lot.
Did Freya mind a little?
Not a little, not a jot.

parfait
(vanilla)

drumstick
(turkey)

pear
(any)

toffee
apple
(Royal Gala)

By Thursday, fussy Freya
was tucked up in her bed.
Her mummy moaned, her daddy groaned.
"This can't go on," Mum said.

"She's turned down all her favourite food.
She's getting very thin.
I'm worried that she'll soon be
nothing more than bones and skin."

skin

bones

Mum, in despair, phoned Grandma Clare.

"You were the same at three,"

said Grandma Clare to Freya's mum.

"Send Freya here to me."

miaow...

So Freya packed her weekend bag

to stay with Grandma Clare,

with pink pyjamas, Monkey Monks

and Kanga and Brown Bear.

"What will you eat for tea, my sweet?"
asked Freya's Grandma Clare.

"I'd like giraffe and warthog
and monkey and brown bear."

"You run away and play, my dear.
We'll whip you up a feast."
"We'll sort her," whispered Grandma Clare,
"the fussy little beast."

Freya played with Grandpa's trains
and grinned a wicked grin.
"Perhaps they'll give me lollipops
and sweeties in a tin."

humbugs etc.

train (expensive)

Freya as
princess

(profile)   (frontal)

Grandpa came dressed as a chef,
a grin upon his face.
"Please come this way, Princess," he said
and led her to her place.

sterling
silver

Upon the table stood a feast,
a fine and splendid spread
of silver salvers, purple plates —
"Ooh, that looks good!" she said.

— fake snake

Zebra hide
(South African)

"You said you'd eat some animals
and then you'd go to bed.
So our first dish is elephant
with egg upon its head."

Grandma laughed a little
and then she laughed a lot.
Did she care when Freya whimpered?
Not a little, not a jot.

"Freya, little darling,
here's **warthog**, if you please.

We serve it here in Norfolk

with a little bit of cheese."

Camembert

Musca domestica

Grandpa laughed a little
and then he laughed a lot.

Did he care when Freya pouted?
Not a little, not a jot.

— mature cheddar
(very mature)

"Freya, precious poppet, here's mashed monkey with fried rice!
We eat it in the summer and we find it very nice."

Freya's lips were quivering –
   she wept and shook her head.

"I really want, I'd really like
   some butter on brown bread."

Grandpa laughed a little
   and Grandma laughed a lot.
"Would you like it served with grilled giraffe
   and cream upon the top?"

boiiing

crocodile
(fake)

Freya caught the train next day
With clever Grandma Clare
and Monkey Monks and Kanga,
her pyjamas and Brown Bear.

genuine leather
(lizard)

tea (Earl Grey)

pie (any)

Freya ate up all her tea –

"That was good," she said.

"I'm not a fussy eater now."

And then she went to bed.

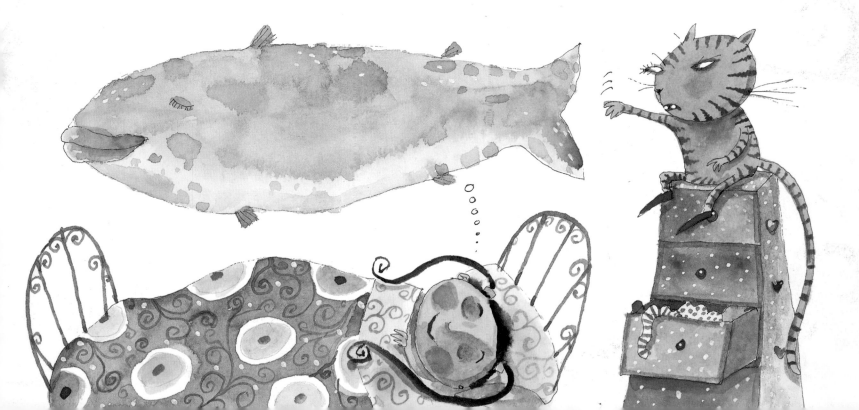

tail (monkey)

wart

And whenever she was fussy,

Dad would ask her in a trice,

"Would you rather eat mashed monkey

on a special bed of rice?

We have it in the freezer

and the warthog's there on ice.

We can heat it in a jiffy

with a sprinkling of spice."

chop baby potatoes

Daddy laughed a little,
Freya laughed a lot.
Did they cuddle just a little?
No, they cuddled quite a lot!

FALKIRK COUNCIL
LIBRARY SUPPORT
FOR SCHOOLS

MORE TITLES FROM FRANCES LINCOLN CHILDREN'S BOOKS

Bubble Trouble
Margaret Mahy
Illustrated by Polly Dunbar

What a terrible thing to lose a baby brother in a bubble!
Follow the hilarious efforts of Mabel and the townsfolk
as they work together to save Baby – and rascal rebel Abel
whose pebble and sling are ready to triple trouble!
Can Mabel and friends save her brother and the day?

Hudson Hates School
Ella Hudson

Hudson doesn't like school. In fact, he HATES it. And most
of all, he hates spelling tests. After another horrible day
Hudson declares he will never go back. But one final very
different test helps Hudson understand what makes him
special and how school can be fun.
A quirky and sensitive treatment of the subject of dyslexia
by an exciting new author/illustrator.

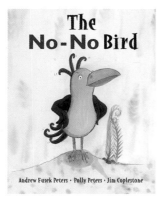

The No-No Bird
Andrew Fusek Peters and Polly Peters
Illustrated by Jim Coplestone

No-No Bird's favourite word is NO!
He says NO to everyone and NO to everything.
NO he won't play with Little Mouse!
NO he won't climb trees with Squirrel!
Then he meets Snake and learns that Snake's favourite
food is No-No Bird. Can No-No Bird escape from a sticky
end by changing his favourite word to YES?

Frances Lincoln titles are available from all good bookshops.
You can also buy books and find out more about your favourite titles,
authors and illustrators on our website: www.franceslincoln.com